NEW HAVEN FREE PUBLIC LIBRARY

W9-AJP-952

DATE DUE

SEP 13 2004		
SEP 0 6 2005	NOV 0 1 2013	
MAY 2 6 2007		
SEP 1 0 2007		
APR	OCT 1 5 2014	
AUG 0 2 2016		

Text © 1997 by Rosemary Wells.
Illustrations © 1997 by Susan Jeffers.

All rights reserved. No part of this book may be reproduced or transmitted in any
form or by any means, electronic or mechanical, including photocopying, record-
ing, or by any information storage and retrieval system, without written permis-
sion from the publisher. For information address Hyperion Books for Children,
114 Fifth Avenue, New York, New York 10011-5690.

Printed in the United States of America.

First Edition
1 3 5 7 9 10 8 6 4 2

Wells, Rosemary. McDuff moves in / Rosemary Wells ; illustrated by Susan
Jeffers. —1st ed.   p.   cm.
Summary: A little white dog that nobody seems to want finds just the right
home—and a name.
ISBN 0-7868-0318-5 (trade)—ISBN 7868-2257-0 (lib. bdg.) [1. Dogs—Fiction.] I.
Jeffers, Susan, ill. II. Title.
PZ7.W4864Mae 1997   [E]—dc20   96-38221

Rosemary Wells

McDuff Moves In

PICTURES BY Susan Jeffers

HYPERION BOOKS FOR CHILDREN
NEW YORK

In the back of a dogcatcher's truck
sat a little white dog nobody wanted.

E WELLS

Thump! went the truck over a bump in the road.
The little dog popped out into the night.

He tumbled onto the soft earth of a tulip bed.
He did not know where he was.

He needed something to eat.
He needed a warm place to sleep.
So he went looking.

"Woof!" said the little white dog at the front door
of number six Pine Road. But the answer from
the other side was, *"GROWL!"*

"Woof!" he said on the front steps of number twelve Oak Lane. But someone said, *"Hiss!"* from the woodpile.

Strange voices hooted and whistled at him
from the trees.

Many pairs of eyes winked and blinked at him from
the darkness of people's gardens.

Rain poured down.
It swirled and swept around him.

Suddenly the wind came up.
It blew the clouds and rain away.

And the moon smiled full on the world. Through an open window in the kitchen of number seven Elm Road wafted the smell of vanilla rice pudding and sausages.

"Woof! Woof! Woof!" said the little white dog.

Nobody growled at him. Nobody hissed at him.
Somebody opened the door and asked him to come in.
It was Lucy. "This is Fred," said Lucy.

No one had ever asked him to come in.
Everyone had always told him to go away.

"What does his collar say?" asked Fred.
"Animal number forty-seven . . . city dog pound," said Lucy.
"He needs help," said Fred.

Lucy spooned out a dish of vanilla rice pudding.
She sliced sausages on top of it. "He's hungry," she said.

After a coconut herbal bath he looked like a snow cloud.
"We certainly can't keep him," Fred said.
"We're much too busy."

"I guess we'll have to take him to the dog pound,"
said Lucy. So they brought him into the car.

Fred drove up and down and around.
"You are going in circles, Fred," said Lucy.

"I don't want to find the dog pound," said Fred.
"I don't want you to find it," said Lucy.

Fred and Lucy brought their new friend home.
"All he needs is a name," said Fred.
They celebrated with hot chocolate.

Lucy opened a tin of McDuff's Melt in Your Mouth
Shortbread Biscuits. "That's it!" said Fred.
"Woof Woof!" said McDuff.

The night was nearly gone.
The rain clattered and spattered over everything.
Lucy and Fred and McDuff fell sound asleep.
"How happy we are!" they said in their dreams.

JAN - 9 1998